Rameau's Nephew

by **Shelley Berc**
and
Andrei Belgrader

From *Le Neveu de Rameau*
by **Denis Diderot**

A SAMUEL FRENCH ACTING EDITION

SAMUEL FRENCH

FOUNDED 1830

New York Hollywood London Toronto

SAMUELFRENCH.COM

IMPORTANT BILLING AND CREDIT REQUIREMENTS

Rameau's Nephew premiered at the CSC Repertory Company in New York City in October 1988. It was directed by Andrei Belgrader, with costumes by Candice Donnelly; lighting by Robert Wierzel; sound by William Uttley, and sets by Anita Stewart. Translation consultant was Holley Stewart.

I......................................Nicholas Kepros
HE.....................................Tony Shalhoub

It was subsequently presented in September 1990 by the American Repertory Theatre with Jeremy Geidt replacing Nick Kepros.

CHARACTERS

I

HE

ACT I

I.

Rain or shine, it is my custom, at five o'clock, in the afternoon, to walk in the Palais Royal. There you can see me on the bench by the Hotel d'Argenson, always alone, always dreaming. I talk to myself about politics, love, art, or philosophy, and give my thoughts full rein, allowing them to chase the first idea, wise or foolish that comes along, just the way teenage boys chase some pretty young thing with her long legs, pert breasts, and a firm behind, then leave her to chase another one, going after them all, but sticking to none. My thoughts are my sluts.

If it is too cold or too wet, I go to the Cafe de la Regence. There I amuse myself watching the chess players.

(A huge vertical panel with chess pieces slides on stage. The pieces appear to be moving alone.)

I was there one afternoon, observing all, speaking to none, and listening as little as possible, when I was approached by one of the weirdest characters in this country of ours where, as we all know, God has given us many. The man I am speaking of is a perfect mix of good sense and lunacy. He has no idea about his good qualities and is totally shameless about displaying his bad ones. Nothing in the world resembles him less than himself. He lives from day to day, happy or sad, ragged or well-dressed, according to circumstance or how he feels.

These originals, I do not like them.

I talk to them once a year when I run into them, because their character is so different. They break the

7

monotony of our politeness and social convention. This kind of man, when he joins a party, is like a grain of yeast, a ferment, which wakes in each something of his natural self.

I have known this particular man for a long time. He always asks me for some money which I usually let him have. You are curious to know the name of this man, and you will know it. His name is Rameau, and he is the nephew of the famous composer Rameau who has created unintelligible visions and apocalyptic theories of music which no one ever reads, who, after having buried the Florentine Lully, will in turn himself be buried by the Italian virtuosi, a fact of which he has a presentiment which tends to make him gloomy and morose, for no one is so irritable—not even a pretty woman who awakes with a pimple on her nose—as an author in danger of surviving his fame.

("I" goes to the chessboard.)

I.
So as I was watching the chess players ...

("HE" enters from behind the chessboard.)

HE.
Aaaah. There you are, Mr Philosopher. And what are you doing here among these sloths, wasting your time pushing the wood?
I.
No. But when I have nothing better to do, it amuses me to watch those who push well.

HE.

In that case, you're not amused too often For, with the exception of Legal and Philidor, all the others play very badly.

I.

It appears you only tolerate men of genius—those who are far above the crowd.

HE.

In chess, art, music, and other nonsense, what good is mediocrity?

I.

Not much, true. Only that many people must dabble in such things before a real genius emerges. But enough of that. I haven't seen you in a long time. I hardly think of you when I don't see you, but when I do see you I'm happy to see you. What have you been up to?

HE.

Same as you and the rest—good, bad, and nothing. I got hungry and ate, when there was food. After eating, I was thirsty and had a drink sometimes. Meanwhile my beard grew and I had a shave.

I.

So, how is your health?

HE.

Usually fine. But not so good today.

I.

Speaking of which, how is your uncle? Have you seen him lately?

HE.

Sometimes I bump into him in the street

I.

Doesn't he ever do anything for you?

HE.

My uncle? Nothing. My tongue could be hanging out a foot and he wouldn't give me a glass of water. He is a philosopher in his own way too. He thinks only of himself. That's what I like about geniuses. They have no idea what it means to be good citizens, fathers, brothers uncles. Men of genius—who needs them? They are the ones who change the face of the world, but even in the smallest thing, public stupidity is so deeply rooted, that along with these changes comes total mayhem. Some of what men of genius dream up gets done, but the rest remains exactly the same. From this, a world more complicated, a Tower of Babel, a mess. Everything gets worse. The true wisdom is: do your duty somewhat, always praise the boss, and let the world go its own sweet way. And it goes pretty well—the majority is satisfied with it. If I knew anything about history, I would show you that evil on Earth has always come from some man of genius. But I don't know shit about history because I don't know shit about anything, and I'll be damned if I'm any worse off for it .

Just last week, I was dining with an important politician. He demonstrated as clear as day that nothing is more useful to the nation than lies and nothing more harmful than truth. I can't quite remember his reasoning, but it followed plainly enough that men of genius are detestable and that if a newborn child bears the mark of this hideous gift of Nature, he should be either smothered or thrown to the wolves.

I.

My dear Rameau, I agree with you that geniuses are somewhat eccentric, but what about Shakespeare?

HE.

What about Shakespeare?

I.

Would you prefer that he had been a silk merchant giving his wife a legitimate baby once a year, a good husband, a good father, good uncle, but nothing more, or that he had been a rogue, a thief, a liar, a profligate, and the creator of *Hamlet, The Tempest, King Lear*?

HE.

Well, for him it would have been better if he had been the former.

I.

What he is saying is truer than he knows!

HE.

Oh, you philosophers! When we say something smart, it is an accident, the word of some inspired idiot.

I.

Why did you say it would have been better for him?

HE.

Because all those fine works he created didn't bring him much money. If he had been a silk merchant, a wholesale grocer or a successful broker, he would have made a lot of money and in doing so would have enjoyed all varieties of pleasure. From time to time, he might have paid some poor dog, like me, to make him laugh or find him a sweet piece of tail to relieve the monotony of living with his old bag of a wife. We would have had big dinners at his home, drunk good wines, great liqueurs, snorted exquisite powders, and sailed to exotic climes. You see, I know what I mean well enough —you laugh—but let me tell you, it would have been better for those around him.

I.

All right, but what if he used his money badly and locked out all your thieves, rogues and pointless people. What if he ordered his shop-boys to beat up any pimp offering variety to husbands sick of their wives?

HE.

Beat him up? Beat him up? People like us do not get beaten up. Not in this day and age. We have laws to protect us. What do you expect people to spend their money on, if not gourmet dinners, expensive wines, pleasures of every kind? But back to Shakespeare. The man was of no use until he was dead.

I.

Agreed. But weigh the good against the bad. A thousand years from now, he will still be revered by people all over the world, will still inspire kindness, compassion, love. So what if he had a few faults and vices ... If everything here below were perfect, nothing would stand out as perfect.

HE.

Crap! To hell with perfection. The only important thing is that you and I are and that we are you and I. I would rather be the poor bastard I am than not exist at all.

I.

People who think like you do not realize they are jeopardizing their own existence.

HE.

I don't understand a word you are saying. It must be philosophy. I'll be honest with you—sometimes, I would like to be someone else, even at the risk of being a genius. Never in my life have I heard one praised without becoming enraged. I am envious. I love to hear terrible things said about the private lives of great men. It brings them closer to me, and helps me to bear my mediocrity. Yes, I have always been and always will be upset with my mediocrity. Yes, yes, I am mediocre and I am upset. I hate my uncle. Something within me says: "Rameau, *you* could have written those two famous pieces of his, and had you done so, they would have been played and sung everywhere. You would walk with your head held high, people would single you out on the street and say, "He is the one who created those great canzones." And the great man Rameau, the Nephew, would fall asleep to a soft murmur of praise ringing in his ears. (*To audience.*) All together now, "Rameau, Rameau ..." Even in his sleep he would smile serenely, and he would snore like a great man.

(RAMEAU lies down at the feet of the audience, closes his eyes, and imitates the happy sleep he imagines.)

I.
So, you think that the rich and famous sleep better.
HE.
Absolutely. When a rich man snores his whole house shakes. Whereas I, Rameau, the nephew, poor outcast that I am, when I go to sleep in my little room, all shrivelled up under my torn blanket, my chest tight, my breathing difficult, only a feeble whine comes out.
I.
Well, that is pretty sad.
HE.
Yes, but what has happened to me is even sadder.
I.
Well, so what has happened?
HE.
You have always taken a certain amount of interest in me because, although I am someone you really despise, I amuse you.
I.
Yes, that is true.
HE.
All right I'll tell you about it. *(HE sighs deeply and puts both hands to his forehead, then HE recovers an appearance of calm and says:)* I was sponging off little Hus, the actress from the Comedie Francaise, and her lover, the financier Bertin. That's where I found my nook. They liked me precisely because I am lazy, gluttonous, and out of my mind.
I.
What credentials.

HE.
And that's not all.
I. (*To the audience.*)
How strange! I always thought that one either hid these things from oneself or else pardoned them in oneself and despised them in others.
HE.
Hide them from oneself? No way. Despise them in others? These people treated me like a king. I was their little Rameau, their crazy Rameau, their impudent Rameau, THEIR Rameau. Each of these epithets brought me a smile, a slap on the back, a kick in the ass. At dinner it brought me a choice cut, and after dinner, certain liberties I could take without them being of any consequence, for I am a man of no consequence. Anybody can do whatever he wants with me, around me, in front of me, on top of me. Who am I to feel insulted? Oh, the gifts they showered on me! What a dog I am to have lost it all! I lost it all because once, just once in my life, I showed common sense. Never, never again!
I.
But what happened?
HE.
"Rameau, Rameau," they grabbed you by the shoulders, showed you the door, "Scram you no-account, and stay out. "It" wants to be sensible; "it" wants to have common sense. We have enough of those qualities without you." I slinked away biting my fingernails. It was my tongue I should have bitten off first.
I.
Is the mistake you made so unforgivable? If I were you, I would go back to these people—they need you more than you think.

HE.
Oh, I am sure that now I am no longer there to amuse them, they're bored to death.

I.
I would not give them time to forget me. However good you are, someone else can always take your place.

HE.
I don't think so!

I.
I would go back right now, just as you are, pale and bleary-eyed, unbuttoned and unkempt, in your present tragic condition. I would throw myself at the feet of the goddess, glue my face to the ground, and still prostrate, say to her in a low, sobbing voice: "Forgive me, my angel, oh, forgive me! I am unworthy, I am a wretch—a victim of a momentary lapse, for as you well know, I am not made for common sense. And I promise you I will never do it again." (*To audience.*) The amusing part of it was that what I said to him, he illustrated in pantomime. He cast himself on his knees, he pressed his face to the ground, pretending to hold the toe of a slipper in his hands. (*HE does so and repeats after "I."*)

I.	**HE.** (*Unintelligibly.*)
He wept ...	(*Weeps.*)
He sobbed ...	(*Sobs.*)
He cried ... Yes, yes my little queen ...	Yes, yes, my little queen ...
I promise ...	I promise ...
Never, never again will I do it ...	Never, never again will I do it ...
Never in my life ...	Never in my life ...

HE.
"Oh, my little queen, I promise never, never to do it again." You're smart. That's the way. She is kind. Everyone says that she is kind. Even I have seen her be kind. But to humiliate myself before that bitch, to grovel at the feet of a second-rate actress who is invariably booed off the stage. Me, Rameau, son of Rameau, the apothecary of Dijon, a man of muster, who never bowed to anyone? Me, Rameau, the nephew of him who is called the great Rameau? Me, Rameau, who has composed sublime pieces of music for harpsichord that no one ever plays? No, sir, I cannot do it!

I. (*To audience.*)
And placing his hand on his heart ...

HE.
I feel something within me rise and say "Rameau, you will not do this. There is a certain human dignity that nothing can erase." It must show up out of the blue because other days, I could be as vile as required. On those days, for a penny, I could kiss little Miss Hus's ass.

I.
I believe you, my friend. It is white, soft, young, dimpled and plump. That is an act of humility that someone more discriminating than you could lower himself to.

HE.
Let's get this straight There is ass kissing literal and ass kissing figurative. What one might relish literally, one could despise figuratively.

I.
If you do not like my suggestion, have the courage to stay poor.

HE.
It is so hard to stay poor when you're surrounded by the rich. Besides, self-loathing becomes unbearable.

I.
What do you know of self-loathing?
HE.
Know of it? How many times have I told myself
"Rameau, in this city, there are people who are rolling in
money, swimming in money, there's money coming out of
their rears, and you're broke, you're broke, you're broke!
Thousands of nobodys without talent, without charm,
running around with fat portfolios and Italian suits and you
go around like this?" What am I, a jerk? Don't I know how
to lie, cheat, swear, manipulate, make promises and break
them? Don't I know how to crawl on all fours? (*As a
pimp.*) Can't I convince a young girl from the provinces
who has just arrived in the city to meet a few influential
men, a few times a week, only in the afternoon, never on
Sunday ...

(RAMEAU plays a Girl and a Pimp.)

(GIRL). Wouldn't it be better if I took a regular job?
(PIMP). No, no one gets anywhere like that, not in this
city.
(GIRL). But what would Daddy say?
(PIMP). Never mind Daddy. First he'll get angry, then
he'll get over it.
(GIRL). But Mommy always taught me that hard,
honest work is everything.
(PIMP). Where have you been, baby? Times have
changed.
(GIRL). And what about my boyfriend on the farm? He
loves me.
(PIMP). He'll love you even more when you show up
in big diamond earrings.
(GIRL). Will I have big diamond earrings?

(PIMP). Yeh—and mink coats, and satin shoes, lace lingerie, chocolate, yachts, caviar, crystal chandeliers, beach front property.

(GIRL). (*Giggling.*) Beach front property?

HE.
Her heart thrills with joy. I stick her in a pied a terre and sit back and take my cut.

What, have a gift like this and go hungry? Millions without my skills are wallowing in wealth and fame, and you think I don't know about self-loathing—the agony caused by the neglect of our natural talent. Better never to have been born at all.

I.
(*To audience.*) As I was watching him act out the scene between the pimp and the young lady, I was torn between two opposing emotions. Whether to abandon myself to laughter or indignation. So insightful and so base, so sincere and so vicious.

HE.
What's wrong?

I.
Nothing.

HE.
You look upset.

I.
I am.

HE.
So what do you think?

I.
Oh, unhappy man, how low you have fallen!

HE.
I didn't mean to depress you. Don't worry—I've saved a little money from my patrons. As I've told you, I had everything I wanted, absolutely everything, and they gave

me an allowance, too. (*HE hits his forehead with clenched fists, bites his lips, rolls his eyes.*) It's over, it's all over.

I.

Are you saying all is lost?

HE.

Lost? No, I wouldn't say that. Money isn't everything. The main thing is to go easily and peacefully every night to the toilet. Oh, priceless shit! That's the great produce of life. When the final hour comes, it's the same for a rich man who leaves twenty seven million and a Rameau who will have a shroud from a public charity. To rot under marble or to rot under dirt is still to rot. Just look at my wrist. It used to be stiff as hell. My fingers were as rigid as wooden sticks. The tendons were like dried-up catgut. But I have so pulled, strained and broken them. (*To hand.*) You won't? I say you will! You will! (*While speaking, with his right hand HE seizes the wrist and fingers of his left and turns them first up and then down. The tips of the fingers touch his arm, the joints crack.*)

I.

Be careful, you could cripple yourself!

HE.

Don't worry. They are used to it. For twenty years, I have given them this kind of treatment. In spite of their stubbornness, the buggers learned to find their place on the keys and on the strings. So now all is well. (*HE flings himself into the pose of a violin player: humming an allegro, his right arm imitating the movement of the bow. His left hand and his fingers feeling along the neck of the violin.*)

I. (*To audience.*)

If he played a false note, he stopped, tightened a string, plucked it with his nail to assure himself it was right, and resumed where he had left off. He beat time with his foot, and worked his head, his hands, his arms and his body like some virtuoso at a concert. Then came a moment of harmony, and his face was transfigured. (*Pause.*) Is it not painful to witness the torment of someone who is so busy depicting pleasure?

HE.

(*Finishing.*) Well, what do you think?

I.

A wonder.

HE.

It's so-so. Sounds just about as good as the others. (*HE crouches down like a musician taking his place at a harpsichord.*)

I.

Please, spare us.

HE.

No, not while I've got you here. You have to listen. I want no one to support me without knowing why. Then you will praise me with more conviction and you just might bring me a student.

I.

I am not well connected. You are wasting your time.

HE.

Don't worry. I don't mind. (*HE plays the nonexistent harpsichord, and makes excited musician noises with his mouth.*)

I. (*To audience.*)

He sat at the harpsichord, his head raised toward the ceiling, where he apparently saw his score. He played, he sang, his fingers flew over the keys. Various passions chased one another across his face—tenderness, anger, pleasure, sorrow. (*Pause.*) I am sure that an abler man than I would have recognized the piece he was playing. The oddest part of the performance was that, from time to time, he would feel for his notes, go back as though he had missed a phrase, and was annoyed that he no longer had the piece at his fingertips.

HE. (*Proudly.*)

Now you can see that we, too, know how to place a tritone, a superfluous fifth, and that the syncopation of dominants is familiar to us. Those enharmonic passages that made my uncle famous are no tremendous feat—we can do them, too.

I.

You've gone to great lengths to prove that you are talented. I was willing to take you at your word.

HE.

Talented? Nooo. In my line of work, I know a little, which is more than is necessary. I ask you, does anyone in this country need to know what he teaches? Now, Master Philosopher, tell the truth. Wasn't there a time when you were not as prosperous as you are now?

I.

I am not very prosperous now.

HE.

Well, you don't sleep on park benches anymore. Do you remember?

I.

Yes, yes, I remember. Let us forget it.

HE.

Covered in rags ...

I.

Yes, yes.

HE.

An old holey overcoat, leaky boots, threadbare pants, a rope for a belt.

I.

Whatever you say.

HE.

In the morning, didn't you teach mathematics?

I.
Without knowing anything about it—that is what you wanted to get out of me, isn't it?

HE.
Yup.

I.
I learned myself by teaching others and I turned out some good students.

HE.
How old is your daughter?

I.
Dammit! Leave my daughter alone!

HE.
In all humility, may one not beg my dear Mr. Philosopher to know how old his daughter might be?

I.
Let us say that she is eight.

HE.
Eight years old! Then for the past four years she should have had her fingers on those keys. Is she to learn no music?

I.
I do not care to include in the scheme of her educations a study that takes so much time and is of so little use.

HE.
Well, what do you teach her?

I.
Grammar, mythology, history, geography, a little drawing and a lot of ethics.

HE.
It would be so easy to prove to you how useless these things are nowadays. Useless—no! Dangerous. But let's forget that. Don't you think she will need a teacher or two?

I.
Of course.

HE.
And do you expect those teachers to know grammar, mythology, history, geography and ethics? Dream on, Mr. Philosopher, dream on. If they knew these subjects well, they wouldn't teach them.
I.
Why not?
HE.
Because they would have been too busy spending their whole lives learning them. Those who know enough to know, know that they don't know.
I.
Such worthy ideas so mixed up with so much nonsense.
HE.
Who knows? The fact is that if you don't know everything you don't know anything well: where something comes from, where something else is going, which one goes first, which follows, how they both fit. What is the cause of phenomenon? What makes the universe tick? It would be better to know nothing than to know so little so poorly. These were the ideas I was toying with when I took up teaching accompaniment and composition.
I.
And you know nothing about either?
HE.
Nada. Zip. Zilch. Bupkis. Not a Goddamn thing. But there are others who are worse than I—those who think they know something. At least I didn't ruin the minds and fingers of my students. When they go from me to a good teacher, since they have learned nothing, they have nothing to unlearn.
I.
How do you do it?

HE.

As they all do. I arrive, and hurl myself into a chair. "Dreadful weather, and the traffic!" Then gossip: (*RAMEAU plays himself and a Mother.*)

(RAMEAU). There's talk of an odd marriage—between Mademoiselle what's-her-name, who used to be kept by ... Uh, uh, uh ... and her lover ... MISS, TAKE YOUR BOOK! She had two, three, children by him, though before him many others ...

(AS MOTHER). Oh, no, Rameau, that can't be!

(RAMEAU). They say they are already married. Mademoiselle Ra-Ra-Ra-... is playing the role of a vestal virgin in a new opera.

(AS MOTHER). But she's six months pregnant, at least!

(RAMEAU). She would listen, and laugh: "He is such a charmer!" Meanwhile the daughter's book would be found under an armchair where it had been dragged by some puppy or kitten. She would sit at the harpsichord and bang away. Then I would go up to her, having nodded my approval to the mother, and since I am supposed to do something, I'd take her hands and rearrange her fingers on the keys. I would lose my temper and scream, "Sol, miss, sol! This is a sol! Do, re, mi, fa, sol!" Then her mother would come to my aid:

(MOTHER). Dumpling, have you no ear? Even I, who know nothing about music, can tell that it is a sol. You are giving your teacher an incredible pain. You don't remember a thing he tells you and you make no progress. (*Bashes imaginary child.*)

(RAMEAU). Forgive me, Madame. It could go better if the young lady would practice a little. But, as it is, it's not too bad.

(MOTHER). If I were you, I'd make her play the same piece over and over again for a year.

(RAMEAU). Don't worry, Madame, I'll make sure that she keeps playing this one until she's mastered it to perfection.

HE.

The hour would pass. I'd grab my fee, and that was called a lesson of accompaniment.

I.

And is it any different today?

HE.

Certainly. Completely. I arrive, I throw off my gloves, I open my harpsichord, I run my fingers over the keys, I am always in a hurry. "BRING IN THE CHILD!" If I am kept waiting even a minute, I yell as if I were being robbed: "In an hour, I have to be at Plaza de Such and Such, in two hours with Madame the Duchesse de So and So, for dinner, I am expected at the House of Marquise de Blah Blah Blah and after that I am due at the concert of Baron de Moula ... WHERE IS THE CHILD?"

I.

All this time no one is expecting you anywhere?

HE.

Right.

I.

Why do you tell all these lies?

HE.

Lies? Lies? I am just employing the standard expressions of trade. Don't they say the bigger the business, the better the man? Don't they also say he who has a good name is worth his weight in gold? There are a lot of people who have a good name but no money. On the other hand, as you know, if you have money you've got your good name. The greatest thing is to have both and that is precisely what I am after when I employ what you call lies. I give good lessons which gives me the good name, and I make believe that I have more students than hours in the day, and that's (*Looks intensely at I, then to members of the audience.*) advertising.

I.

And do you really give good lessons?

HE.

Yes ... not bad ... Er ... umm ... Well, so-so. In the old days I used to steal my students' money, now I earn it.

I.

And did you steal it with no remorse?

HE.

None. The parents were rolling in money. They're bankers, brokers, wholesalers, city commissioners. Together with all the rest they had to employ, I merely helped them make restitution. In Nature, all species prey on each other. In society we do the same. It's called Service Economy.

I.

What about your conscience?

HE.

What conscience? The voice of conscience is very weak when one has needs. Isn't it enough that when I get rich, I'll have to make restitution, too? And I am prepared to do it in every way. Gorging, gambling, guzzling, womanizing ... shopping.

I.

I am afraid you'll never get rich.

HE.

I sometimes doubt it myself.

I.

But for argument's sake, let us assume that fortune smiles and you do get rich, what then?

HE.

I will be the most shameless motherfucker ever. I love bossing people around and I will boss them. I love praise, and they will praise me. I will get myself a whole gaggle of artists and intellectuals, on salary, and say to them "Come on dogs, entertain me," "Rip apart all those decent people." We will eat, drink, poke, commit exquisite perversities, and tell dirty stories about great men and philosophers.

I.

Seeing the way you'd use your riches, I can see how much we are losing with you being a beggar.

HE.

You think that happiness is the same for everyone. What a strange idea! It assumes a certain singularity of mind that is not ours. Do you think what you call virtue is for everyone? The few who have it, let them keep it. Just imagine for a moment a universe sage and philosophical. Honestly, wouldn't it be an unbelievable bore? Let me tell you the real wisdom of Solomon: drink fine wines, stuff yourself with delicacies, bury yourself in luscious flesh, and lounge on designer sheets; all else is vanity.

I.

What about love for one's country?

HE.

Vanity! There are no countries left! All I see from pole to pole are tyrants and slaves.

I.

What about helping one's friends?

HE.

No one has any friends. And even if one has, why risk making them ungrateful by helping them?

I.

What about duty?

HE.

What duty?

I.

Duty toward society!

HE.
What do you get from that? Envy, trouble, persecution.
Now is that any way to get on in this world?
I.
What about educating your children?
HE.
That's the school's business.
I.
But what if the teachers are just like you—who do you
think is going to suffer?
HE.
Not me.
I.
But what if these children grow up to become thieves
and drug addicts?
HE.
Then they're society's problem.
I.
Wouldn't that disgrace you?
HE.
Nothing could disgrace me if I were rich.
I.
At least you would watch over your wife's conduct?
HE.
Not on your life. The best you can do for your better
half is to let her do whatever she wants. Don't you think
the world would be a better place if everyone minded his
own business?
I.
I agree. When I do my job well, I am at peace with the
whole world.
HE.
I know just what you mean.

I.
And it's not that I despise the pleasure of the senses; I have a palate, too and it is tickled by a delectable wine or dish. I have a heart, and eyes, too; I like to see a pretty woman, to feel the firm curve of her breasts in my hand, to press her lips to mine, to drink bliss from her eyes, and pass out in the cradle of her hips. Sometimes, I enjoy a lively party even when it gets a little rowdy. But I must confess that I find it infinitely more pleasurable to help the needy, give sensible advice to a friend, spend an instructive hour with my child, or write a good page of prose.

HE.
Do you think we should all be decent people?

I.
Yes. If we want to be happy.

HE.
I see a lot of decent people who are not happy, and a lot of people who are happy but not decent.

I.
So it seems to you.

HE.
Isn't it because I showed common sense and decency for one second, that I have nowhere to sleep tonight?

I.
Not at all. It is for not having shown common sense and decency all the time. You should have found a way to make a living without being a dependent leech.

He.
Leech or not, my way is the easiest.

I.
And the least secure and the least decent.

HE.
But the most consistent with my nature which is lazy, servile, and crooked.

I.
I can't argue there.
HE.
Since I can make myself happy by indulging in vices that are natural to me and congenial to the habits of my countrymen, it would be wrong to twist and torment myself into a virtuous shape. I would become deformed. I would suffer. And when you suffer, you make other people suffer, too. In short, I don't want the kind of happiness that visionaries like you dream up.
I.
I see, my dear friend, that you don't understand it, and obviously are not made for it.
HE.
Thank God for that. It would only make me starve to death and die of boredom.
I.
After all this, I can only recommend that you go back to the place from which you so carelessly allowed yourself to be kicked out.
HE.
And do to Miss Hus what you do not object to literally, but which is a little repugnant to me figuratively?
I.
That is my opinion.
HE.
Let's get this straight. I am perfectly willing to grovel but not on command. I have absolutely no problem giving up my dignity. You are laughing?
I.
Your dignity makes me laugh.
HE.
Go ahead, laugh. But let me tell you that everybody has his own kind. I'm willing to forget mine—when I feel like it. I was kicked around by Bertin and right now I don't feel

like going back for more. Besides, you have no idea what a looneybin that house is. Imagine, a melancholy and morose old man, eaten up by neurosis, his yellow bathrobe wrapped around him three times. Imagine him, grim and stone-faced, in the middle of my hilarious routines. Between us, the old fart Bertin, with all his awards and citations, is a nobody compared to me. Will he laugh or not? Will he laugh or not? That's what I have to worry about twenty-four hours a day and that is bad for my talent. That hypochondriac, with his skull stuffed into a nightcap pulled over his eyes. You keep waiting for God himself to pull his jaws open. And when his mouth finally moves he says things that make you gag and prove all your art was for nothing: "Yes, Miss, yes, we need Finesse."

I.
Finesse?

HE.
Across the table is Miss Hus who is putting on her usual airs. You might say she's pretty, for she still is, despite a few lumps on her face and a tendency to resemble an obese cow. Now, I like flesh when it's pretty, but matter needs motion. Item: she is meaner, prouder, dumber than a peacock. Item: she thinks she is witty. Item: you have to persuade her that she is wittier than anyone else. I say things like "How amazing! How do you do it? You're such a natural! Don't tell me that experience, education and reflection could improve ... Such genius! What intuition!" and similar stupidities all day long. And ten times a day I have to kneel down, one knee in front of the other, arms outstretched to the Goddess ... That god damn witch's tit of a toad-humping bitch of an elephant-whore.

I.
I didn't know you had to work so hard.

HE.
Not really. I began by watching and copying others.
Maybe doing a better job at it because I'm more shameless.
And I have a better set of lungs. Listen.
I. (*To audience.*)
Then just to give an idea of his pulmonary strengths, he
begins to cough.

*(After a pause, "HE" has an enormous coughing spell. HE
coughs every way imaginable for several minutes.)*

I.
What use is this talent?
HE.
Can't you guess?

End of ACT I

ACT II

MUSIC. LIGHTS up on ACTORS in same position as end of Act I. "HE" resumes 'short' cough.

I.
So what use is this talent?
HE.
You still haven't guessed?
I.
I am a little slow.
HE.
All right, imagine there is an argument going on, and no one knows who will win. I get up and yell, "Yes, yes, it is exactly as Mademoiselle states it! What powers of reason! I defy any of our great minds to come near it. The very form is impeccable." Of course you mustn't always praise her the same way—it would lack style. So I also employ a melodious tone, accompanied by smiles and an infinite variety of faces expressing approval. No one is better at this than I. I approve with my nose, my mouth, my eyes, my chin, my hair. And I have a way of writhing, of twisting my spine, shrugging my shoulders, dropping my head to one side, shutting my eyes, of being thunderstruck. Just look. (*HE demonstrates.*) The contortions of my back, are a Rameau original, needless to say plagiarized by the envious.
I.
I believe you have brought the art of debasement to its utmost heights.

HE.

I told you I am the best. Unfortunately, after a number of brilliant innovations, one is bound to repeat himself. Only God and a handful of geniuses can always come up with something new. Bouret is one of those. His Trick of the Lap Dog overwhelmed and humbled me. Just thinking about it makes me want to give up my art.

I.

What do you mean "The Trick of the Lap Dog"?

HE.

Where have you been? Do you mean to tell me you don't know how Bouret, the Businessman, who wanted a government contract, transferred the affections of his little lap dog from himself to the City Mayor, who had taken a liking to the beast?

I.

I confess I am ignorant of the matter.

HE.

It amazed all Europe! Now Mr. Philosopher, how would you have gone about it? Remember, Bouret's dog loves him. Bear in mind that the dog is afraid of the Mayor and his strange robe. And don't forget, Bouret only had eight days to solve the problem. You must know all the data to appreciate the elegance of his solution. Well?

I.

I freely admit that I am not good at solving puzzles of this kind.

HE.

Listen, listen and drool! (*HE taps him on the shoulder for he has grown familiar.*) Bouret has a mask made in the likeness of the Mayor. With the help of his valet, he borrows the Mayor's robe. He puts on the mask and the robe. He calls the dog, pats him and gives him a biscuit. Then he takes off his disguise. He is no longer Bouret the Mayor, he is again himself, Bouret the Businessman. He calls the dog, and this time he beats it to a pulp. After a couple of days of this routine, the dog runs from Bouret, the Businessman, and runs to Bouret, the City Mayor. But how can you appreciate such artistry, you're just a layman.

I.

You are right.

HE.

To borrow the robe and the wig, I had forgotten the wig! And the mask! It's the mask that makes me green with envy. That's what I call genius. No wonder he made it big. The mask! The mask—I would've give the fingers off my right hand to have had that idea.

I.

But my dear Rameau, you can use the idea yourself! So what if Bouret invented it. You shouldn't be ashamed to "borrow" it.

HE.

I hadn't thought of that. As a matter of fact, it is better to imitate great things than create mediocre ones. But it still bugs me that geniuses are born, not made. Caesar, Moliere, Copernicus, Bouret. Do you think Bouret had to learn how to be great? Ah! When I was born, what greatness did I get?

I.

Well, in spite of the wretched, vile, miserable and abominable part you play, I believe that deep down you have a certain delicacy of soul.

HE.

Not at all. I've none of that. I never lie when it's in my interest to tell the truth, I never tell the truth if it's better to lie. I use freedom of speech for all its worth.

I.

Well, at least his observations on the human character are amazingly precise, at times ... I like them.

HE.
You see, you can learn a lot from bad company, just like from debauchery. And it's not just that—I've done some reading.

I.
What have you read?

HE.
Moliere.

I.
Admirable and instructive.

HE.
But what kind of instruction, that is the point.

I.
Knowledge of duty, love of virtue, hatred of vice.

HE.
Not the way I see it! His plays show me what to do and what not to say. When I read *The Miser*, I said to myself: Be a miser if you want, but don't talk like one. When I read *Tartuffe*: Be a hypocrite if you choose, but don't sound like one. Don't show off your vices, or you will become the object of ridicule. Although, when I think about it, for every time it is necessary to avoid being ridiculous, there are a hundred times when being ridiculous has its advantages. In any event, when it comes to morality, nothing is absolutely true or false, except that one must be what self-interest makes him—good or bad, respectable or ridiculous, honest or full of vice. If virtue, by chance, led to liquid assets, I would be virtuous. As for vice, Nature took care of that. You know what I mean?

I.
This is all very profound but let us get back to your misfortune.

HE.
Misfortune—what misfortune?

I.
The loss of your bread and butter!
HE.
I forgot myself for a moment. Yesterday, Bertin invited Vendome, the Great Poet, may the devil shrivel his pen, to dine. They placed him at the head of the table as the guest of honor. There weren't enough chairs so I ended up on a kitchen stool—that comes up to here (*HE gestures to this knees.*)—way down at the end of the table. Well, over dessert, I yell up to Vendome: "Today, you're in the seat of honor, but tomorrow when the New Great Poet arrives, you will have to move down one seat to your left, the day after tomorrow a Greater Poet than the new Great Poet will arrive and you will have to move down another seat to your left, then an even Greater Great Poet will force all the Great Poets to leave their chairs and you will have to move down yet another seat and so on, from poet to poet, from chair to chair till you take your place by me on some miserable stool from the kitchen! 'Come un cazzo maestoso fra due coglioni.'" (*To audience.*) Like a huge dick, between two balls. The Poet laughed, everyone else laughed, except my boss who was furious. He said things that wouldn't have mattered if there hadn't been so many people listening.

(*RAMEAU plays himself, BERTIN and MISS HUS.*)

(BERTIN). Rameau, you are rude!
(RAMEAU). I know, that's why you keep me.
(BERTIN). Rameau, you are a bum.
(RAMEAU). If I weren't, would I be here?
(BERTIN). Rameau, I will have you removed.
(RAMEAU). After dinner, I'll leave myself.

HE.

So we dined, and I cleaned my plate. Then I made up my mind to go. I had given my word in front of so many people that I had to keep it. I prowled up and down the room for a long time, looking for my hat in places where it was not likely to be, waiting for someone to patch things up. Miss Hus approached.

(RAMEAU) But Mademoiselle, was I any different today than usual?

(BERTIN). I want him out.

(HUS). Come Rameau, be a good boy, ask the Poet's pardon.

HE.

Mademoiselle took me by the hand and dragged me to Vendome's seat. I kneeled down and said, "Come un cazzo maestoso fra due coglioni. All this is very silly, isn't it?" I started laughing and he did, too. He obviously accepted my apologies, but I still had to deal with my boss.

(BERTIN). Not another word. I've put up with him long enough.

HE.

I stood there thinking, "Dammit, doesn't he know I am like a child? And that now and then what's inside me has to come out. Even an organ grinder's monkey needs a rest once in a while. I have to entertain them, granted, but I have to have some fun too." In the middle of this mess, I had a sinister thought, a thought that filled me with arrogance and pride—"they can't do without me, I'm irreplaceable."

I.

I agree that you are useful to them, but they are even
more useful to you. It will be difficult for you to find
another home like that; but for every clown they lose, a
hundred more are waiting in the wings.

HE.

A hundred like me? I kept them in stitches day and
night.

I.

And in exchange, you had food, shelter, clothing and
pocket money.

HE.

That's the good side. But you don't say anything about
my duties. For example, when there was a rumor of a new
play, it was my job to sniff out the author and hint that
one of the parts was perfect for a certain actress I knew.

(RAMEAU plays himself and AUTHOR.)

(AUTHOR). And who is that, please?
(RAMEAU). I would whisper Miss Hus's name.
(AUTHOR). That one?
(RAMEAU). "Yes, that one!" I would say, blushing a
little because even I can feel shame once in a while.

HE.

It was even worse when she got the part. Then I had to
go to the theatre. Before getting to the house of torment, I
had to memorize all the insipid passages where I had to lead
the applause. I'd stand up amid the booing public (who are
good judges no matter what the critics say), and clap my
hands, drawing to myself the hisses that should have been
directed at her. And I had to listen to them whisper: "He's
the scumbag that belongs to the man who sleeps with her."
After awhile, I became known and people used to say, "Oh!

It's only Rameau." And then Miss Hus started to get fat.
You should hear the stories about her. Here's a good one—
  At 5:00 in the morning, there were cries of a man being
suffocated. "Help, help I can't breathe! I'm dying!" It was
Bertin. That huge creature Hus, out of her mind with
ecstasy, was going at him full tilt, lifting herself up and
dropping herself down on old limp genitals with all her
two hundred and eighty-five pounds. It was almost
impossible to get him out. Can you believe such a little
hammer sticking itself under such a big anvil?
  I.
I hope you don't help spread these stories.
  HE.
Why not?
  I.
Because it is indecent to ridicule one's benefactors.
  HE.
When people decide to associate with someone like me
they should expect to be treated viciously. If you take a
young provincial to the zoo at Versailles and he is dumb
enough to put his hand between the bars of the tiger's cage,
who is to blame? The tiger? One should not accuse others
of wickedness, rather one should accuse oneself of
stupidity.
  I.
You are right, but let's talk about something else. Ever
since we began, I have had a question on the tip of my
tongue.
  HE.
Why have you held it back so long?
  I.
I was afraid of being indiscreet.
  HE.
After all I have told you?

I.
Well, I was wondering if you could guess my opinion
of you.

HE.
Certainly. Sure. In your eyes, I am the most abject,
despicable creature alive. Sometimes I think the same, but
not too often.

I.
But why show yourself to me in all your turpitude?
Depravity?

HE.
Because if there is one thing in which it is essential to
excel, it is in evil. We despise a small-time mugger but we
can't deny a certain respect for the great criminal. His
daring amazes us, his atrocities thrill. Above all else,
people admire consistency of character.

I.
But you have not yet attained consistency of character. I
find you at times vacillating in your principles. Also it is
uncertain whether you get your evil from Nature or from
study, and whether you have pursued your study as far as
you can go.

HE.
Hey, I'm doing my best.

I.
He then composed in his honor a Song of Triumph. An
eccentric fugue, whose melody was at one moment solemn
and majestic, at another frivolous and light. Listening, I
perceived he had a better understanding of good music than
good morals.

HE. (*Singing.*)
Oh! Earth, receive my gold, guard my treasure. My
soul, my soul, my life ... I am your little friend, your little
friend. No answer? No one's coming. I am waiting, no

one's coming. "Aspettare e non venire" ... I am waiting, no one's coming ...

I.

Did I admire him? Yes, I admired him. Was I moved to pity? Yes, I was moved to pity, but a touch of ridicule suffused my feelings and tainted them.

I.

He worked himself into a frenzy, and performed twenty different roles, with chorus and orchestra. He was a woman swooning in grief, a man sunk in despair, a young girl discovering the pangs of love, a prophet bemoaning the destruction of Jerusalem; he was a babbling brook, a giant waterfall, a hurricane, an earthquake, a temple being erected, birds twittering at sunset, the cries of the dying mingled with howling winds and the crash of thunder. He was a night with all its darkness, gloom, and silence, for silence, too, can be depicted in sound.

HE.

What is it? Why do you laugh? Why are you surprised? This is music and this is the musician. I defy anyone to play "Aspettare e non venire" better.

I.

He looked around and wiped his face mechanically, like a man who wakes to find a crowd around his bed and doesn't remember what has happened.

("HE" sits, leans his head against the wall, arms dangling, eyes half closed.)

HE.

I don't know what's wrong with me. When we started, I felt great, I was rested, in good shape, and now I am beat ... It came on very suddenly.

I.

Can I get you a drink?

HE.
Thanks. I feel like somebody hit me over the head, I am a little weak, and my chest hurts. This happens to me almost every night. I don't know why.
I.
What will you have?
HE.
Whatever. At the rate we're going, I have no idea what will happen to art. Let's drink.

(Table with two glasses and a bottle slides on stage. The glass is tricked to allow the actor to appear to drink a lot. RAMEAU drinks about ten glasses. "I" swipes the bottle.)

I.
How is it that you can be so finely attuned to the beauties of music and yet so deaf to the beauties of morality?
HE.
It must be that morality is a sense I lack. A string that was not given to me, a loose string that one can pluck forever and never get a sound, or maybe I have hung out with good musicians and bad men. And then, there's genetics. Oh! The cursed paternal molecule!
I.
Do you love your child?
HE.
Will you do nothing to try to stop the effect of the cursed paternal molecule?
HE.
I don't know. What if the molecule wants to turn him into a derelict like his father, then my efforts to turn him into an honest man would go against the natural bent of the molecule and he would be pulled in two directions at

once. Left alone he'd be very good at being bad. But if forced to be good, he wouldn't be very good at being good or bad. Right now I leave him alone. I just watch him. (*Proudly.*) He is already greedy, lazy, and a liar. I'm afraid it runs in the family.

I.

And will you make him a musician so the likeness will be complete?

HE.

A musician! A musician! A musician! Sometimes I look at him, I bare my teeth and I growl, "If you ever learn one single note in your whole life, I will wring your neck."

I.

But why, if you don't mind telling me?

HE.

Because music gets you nowhere. This is what I teach my child whenever I have some loose change in my pocket, which is not often. I plant myself in front of him, and pull out a coin. I raise my eyes toward Heaven, I kiss the coin and lower it in front of his nose. To make him better understand the importance of this sacred piece, I coo and I point with my finger to all the things he can buy with it—a little overcoat, a teddy bear, cookies. Then I replace the coin in my pocket, parade proudly up and down, I raise my coattails, and I smack my hand where the money is. This is the way I teach him that IN THIS WORLD, I-F Y-O-U H-A-V-E M-O-N-E-Y Y-O-U H-A-V-E E-V-E-R-Y-T-H-I-N-G.

I.

But there are people who do not consider wealth the most important thing in life.

HE.

No one is born thinking that way. It's unnatural. Everything that lives, man included, seeks its well-being, at the expense of whoever is in the way. I am sure that if I left my little savage to his own devices, he would one day want to dress elegantly, eat in the best restaurants, travel first class, and be feared by men and lusted after by women.

I.

I am afraid that if your little savage is left to himself and his native imbecility, one day he might join the infant's reasoning to the grown man's passion—strangle his father and sleep with his mother.

HE.

Every moral principle has its drawbacks.

I.

I think I like you better as a musician than as a moralist. Tell me, how is it that with your remarkable faculty for feeling and rendering the most intriguing musical compositions, you yourself have done nothing worthwhile?

HE. (*Starts nodding his head and lifts a finger to heaven.*)

The stars! The stars! When Nature fashioned Bach, Vivaldi, Albinoni, she smiled; but when she belched up Rameau the Nephew, she made a face, (*HE shows contempt.*) another face (*Disgust.*) and another face. (*Disdain.*)

(*HE paces, his head lowered, looking pensive and worried. HE sighs, weeps, despairs, throws up his eyes and hands to heaven, striking his forehead with his fists hard enough to break his knuckles.*)

HE.

I keep thinking there's something there, but I shake it, I beat it, nothing comes out.

(HE shakes his head again and beats it much harder than before, and finally gives up.)

HE.
Either nobody is home, or they don't wanna answer.

(A moment later HE raises his head, assumes a more dignified bearing, places his right hand on his heart and says:)

HE.
But I feel, yes I feel ...

(Sad and in a trance, HE walks off stage. "I" approaches the audience and very calmly:)

I.
He discoursed on the subjects of anger, compassion, hatred, and love, outlining the character of each passion with astonishing accuracy and subtlety. Then he stopped and assumed the attitude of a poor man worn out with fatigue, ready to die if no one throws him a crust of bread. He depicted his extreme need by a silent gesture of a finger pointing to his open mouth. It was as if he were saying "How can one nourish great thoughts, do great works, in the midst of such misery?"

(RAMEAU comes back in a great mood. Happily to the audience:)

HE.
Today the world's your oyster, tomorrow you're down and out. Circumstance guides us, and does it very badly.
I.
My dear Rameau, this is the natural order of things.

HE.

If I have to go hungry and homeless, I want no part of your natural order of things. It's this goddamn economy! Everyone keeps telling me how great things are, yes, some people have it all, while others fight over the garbage. A man with no money doesn't talk, he crawls, he shakes, he stumbles, he cringes. I call it the beggar's pantomime.

I.

No, my dear Rameau, it is the pantomime of all human kind. Even a king finds himself from time to time under the heel of a dainty foot that makes him perform a bit of pantomime. Whoever in this world has need of another has to strike a pose. An officer postures to his general, the general postures to the industrialist, the industrialist postures to the bank and so on and so forth. Really what you call the beggar's pantomime is what makes the world go around. Everyone in this world has his own Bertin and little Hus.

HE.

That cheers me to no end.

I.

There is however one human being who is exempt from posturing: the philosopher who has nothing and wants nothing.

HE.

Where do you find such an animal? If he has nothing, he must be suffering. If he asks for nothing he will get nothing and so he will continue to suffer.

I.

Diogenes the Cynic laughed at these needs.

HE.

But he had to have clothes.

I.

No, he went naked.

HE.
But wasn't it cold in Athens?
I.
Less than here.
HE.
But he had to eat.
I.
No doubt.
HE.
At whose expense?
I.
Nature's.
HE.
An inferior menu.
I.
But abundant.
HE.
Bad service though. And don't you think your philosopher had to at least posture for a piece of ass?
I.
Wrong again. Others paid dearly for the courtesans who gave themselves to him for nothing.
HE.
But what if the courtesan was with a paying customer and Diogenes was in a hurry?
I.
Then he calmly returned to his barrel and did without.
HE.
You want me to do that?
I.
I think it is a lot better to do without than to humiliate and prostitute oneself.
HE.
From what you say, my poor little wife was something of a philosopher too. She had the courage of a lion.

Sometimes we had no bread and no money. I would wrack my brain to think of someone who would lend me money that I would never repay. She, happy as a lark, would sit down at the harpsichord, singing as she played—she sang like a nightingale—I wish you could have heard her. When we were going to play a concert, I would say to her as we went along, "Come, my love, get yourself admired, deploy your talents and your charms: intoxicate and drive them wild." And she would sing, intoxicate and drive them wild. Alas! I lost her, the poor, little one! She not only had talent, she had a perfect mouth, so tiny you could barely put your little finger in it, teeth like a row of pearls, and her eyes, her skin, her breasts ... She had legs like a race horse and a behind fit to sculpt. Sooner or later, she would have hooked a millionaire. How she walked, what hips, my God, what hips! (*HE imitates his wife's walk, HE runs with little steps, holds his head high, flirts and wiggles his behind.*) I paraded her everywhere, the Tuileries, the Palais Royal, the Boulevards. When she crossed the street in the morning with her hair down and in a light short skirt, you would have stopped to look at her and wanted to touch her. The men who followed her watched her firm legs and eyed her shapely hips. She'd let them catch up to her. Suddenly she'd turn on them. Her great, dark, glowing eyes stopped them in their tracks. For the head was as good as the tail. But alas! I lost her and all my dreams of fortune vanished with her. I only married her for that. She knew all my plans—she was too intelligent not to see how fool-proof they were and she had too much judgment not to approve them. (*HE sobs and chokes.*) No, no, there's no consolation for me. I will forever be in mourning .Oh! If only I'd had a daughter... What time is it? I have to go to the theatre.

I.
What are they playing?

HE.
Something of Diderot's. There are some good things in it. What a shame he wasn't the first to write them. Among the dead there are always a few to annoy the living. Can't be helped. Goodbye, Mr. Philosopher ... Isn't it true that I am always the same?
I.
Unfortunately, my dear Rameau, yes.

(MUSIC starts.)

HE.
Unfortunately? I wouldn't say that. He who laughs last...

*("HE" laughs as he exits, then bursts into coughing. "I" smiles and shrugs to audience, and leaves.
MUSIC swells.)*

End